Fizzy's Christmas Tail.

Based on a true story
By
Sarah A. Newbery

Dedicated to Thea, Serena
and Alfie James

To Paul, with my heartfelt love.

Most of all, my thanks to Fizzy Pop, our
loyal rescue dog who inspired this book,
and all the dogs out in the world who just
want to share their love!

Chapter 1.

It was a cold winter's morning and Fizzy was snuggled up in bed with her mum. Fizzy had two brothers and two sisters, the other puppies were all much bigger than her. They went off to play around the kitchen, they played much rougher games than Fizzy, who preferred to snuggle up and cuddle with her mum beside the fire!

"I love you Fizzy." said her mum, "But you need to learn to play with your brothers and sisters, you need to be strong, because someday, you will go to a new family, and I won't be here to cuddle you."

Fizzy was very sad. She loved to cuddle up to her mum, she loved the warmth and smell of her, and loved the feeling of mums soft smooth hair next to her little body, but she knew that she wouldn't be able to stay forever with her family. Mum licked her behind her ear, Fizzy loved this, it made her feel tickly, and most of all, it made her feel loved.

Days went on and winter set in. It began to get cold. Each day, the puppies would be taken from mum in the morning and put outside in the garden to explore for a short while. Fizzy hated this, all she wanted was to cuddle up in front of the fire, and just to be with mum.

Each day the house looked different. Every day boxes and cards would arrive for the family, mum said that soon there would be a special holiday, and these parcels were for the children and family to give to each other, there may even be a gift in there for the puppies, one day soon it would be Christmas day.

"Christmas is awesome," said mum. "We all have to go to bed early, we put carrots on the table for reindeer, and mince pies for Santa, we even leave a glass of milk for him, he's a very busy man and needs lots of energy for his work delivering presents to the children."

"In the night," said mum "I always sleep beside the fire in the kitchen. Because I'm a light sleeper, I hear Santa coming, it's really amazing, first of all I hear the sound of bells over the house, these are the bells attached to his sleigh. The reindeer make a big noise when they land on the roof of the house, but I know I must not bark, or I will scare Santa away and he won't be able to deliver the presents to the children. I lie still in my bed, but I always have one eye open just to take a peep at him!"

"When Santa comes down the chimney, I wag my tail, just a little bit, I can't help myself it's always so exciting!"

"First he fills the stockings for the children that have been put beside the fireplace, he works so fast and he knows just what each child needs. Then he quickly eats his pie and milk, he grabs the carrots, and within seconds, he's gone back up the chimney to the next house."

"The children get up nice and early, they're always so happy, there is lots of laughter, and we get to have extra treats, we even get to sit on the sofa and eat special bones that the family buy."

Fizzy was excited about Christmas, she wasn't sure who Santa was, but he sounded like a very kind man, if not a little busy. She liked the idea of playing with the children all day, the children in her house were so kind to her, when they got in from school, they played with her, and gave her toys and a big fuss.

Chapter 2.

A few nights later, all the puppies were snuggled with mum in her bed.

"Puppies, I have something tell you, you must listen carefully and not say a thing, because what I have to say is very important, and you must remember every word."

The puppies sat up and stared at mum. Her eyes glistened with sadness as she sat up straight to talk to them all, she looked serious, and very very sad.

"It's really important..." she continued, "Really really important that you learn to use your beautiful big eyes to show people you love them, just like this." Mum opened her eyes as widely as she could and stared down with the most amazing love at her puppies.

I get this. thought Fizzy.

"And your ears my babies..." said mum, "Use your ears to show people you're listening to them" Mum lifted up her flappy ears, just a little bit to show the puppies what to do.

One by one, the puppies all tried to lift up their ears, just like mum. *People will love my ears thought Fizzy, they're just like mums and she has the most beautiful ears*.

"Then my children, with your wide eyes looking straight at each other to show love, and your lifted ears to show you're listening, you then tip your head to the side so show that you're cute and that you care about people. This shows the kindness in you, it shows off your heart and your love and will help you find a wonderful new family."

"Finally my children," mum turned around to show her beautiful fluffy tail. She stood up on her short stubby legs, and started to wag it.

"Wag your tail like this my children." she said, "This needs a little practise, but wag it as hard as you can, and this will show your new family the happiness and joy you feel from being with them, go on puppies, wag your tail until your whole body moves with it."

Fizzy stood up, she turned around to realise that indeed she also had a beautiful shaggy tail, just like mum. She'd not taken much notice of it before because, there's so much to think of when you're a puppy. There it was right at the end of her body. She started to wag.

To start with her tail wouldn't move that much, but she kept an eye on it and really concentrated on moving it from left to right, and then right to left, and back again. All of a sudden, her tail was wagging so much that it made her fall off of her stubby little legs and she rolled over onto the cold tiled floor. Her brothers and sisters were laughing at her.

Mum trotted over to her and nuzzled her to get up. "Come on Fizzy my darling, we can try again tomorrow… you have a good heart my baby, and you will find love."

Just at that moment, there was a commotion at the doorway. The children and their father arrived with an enormous Christmas tree. It was so huge, it could hardly fit in the doorway! They carried it through the kitchen into the lounge and put it in the corner to the side of the fireplace.

The children were laughing and singing, as they gathered lots of beautiful decorations and put them on the branches, some were shiny, some were sparkly, and some were made by the children from fun things they'd found around the house. The puppies were allowed in the room to look at the tree but, only with a human there to keep an eye on them!

The branches of the tree were prickly but, smelt really lovely. Fizzy tried to grab one in her mouth and squealed when it hurt her. Her mum raced in as one of the children scooped her up into their arms. They carried her out and closed the door. The Christmas tree was indeed, very special!

It was the week before Christmas, snow had set in on the mountain hills, Fizzy's mum was sad. Four of her puppies had been taken this week, she knew that they had gone to good families. She was sure that they would have a great life but, Fizzy was still so small. Fizzy's mum wanted to keep her cuddled up to her forever, but she knew that she would soon leave too.

And so it was, on Christmas Eve, that a man came to the house.

He seemed like a good man, he talked to the family for a little while. Fizzy's mum explained very quickly to Fizzy that she was going to her own new family, and that she would always be in her heart. Mum licked her a fond farewell behind the ear as Fizzy was picked up and put into a box the man had with him.

The man lifted the box up and wished them all a merry Christmas.

"Goodbye Mr Green" shouted Fizzy's family from the door, the children were touching their eyes, as if to wipe away a tear. Fizzy's mum looked up to her family. The human children were all very sad that Fizzy had gone, they picked up Fizzy's mum and gave her a big cuddle.

Chapter 3.

Fizzy was scared and cold. It was really dark. Mr Green carried the box that Fizzy was in, and plonked it on the seat of the car and then she heard the door slam. The drive in the car seemed to take a long long time. Fizzy wondered how her mum was, and how her human family were preparing for Christmas. She wondered if she would see Santa tonight in her new home.

The car stopped, and Fizzy slid forwards in her box which went tumbling to the floor of the car with a bang. Fizzy squealed as she hurt her ear.

"Oh shush" shouted Mr Green, "Be quiet, I have to keep you a secret."

Fizzy stayed quiet as she felt Mr Green lifting her box out of the car. It was dark inside, with just a little hole for her to peep through. The house in front of her eyes was amazing, it was a huge house with a lovely big garden. The house was covered in beautiful Christmas lights that twinkled like stars.

WOW thought Fizzy - *this is just the most amazing home ever, sure I'm going to be loved here!*

Mr Green carried Fizzy's box to the side of the house and opened up the door of a little wooden shed.

"You'll stay here for the night." he said to Fizzy, "Now no noise at all - do you hear me, or you'll spoil the surprise."

Mr Green left Fizzy with a pink blanket to lie on, and a bowl of water to drink.

This was not the way Fizzy imagined her first Christmas would be! *I should be lying beside the fire in the kitchen with my mum, with one eye open waiting for Santa* thought Fizzy. *I should be watching the children put out the pies and milk, singing and dancing, I just want my mum!*

Fizzy cried, but just quietly, she didn't want Mr Green shouting at her for spoiling the surprise, really she wanted her mum. She was cold with just the blanket, and no one to snuggle to, but she was tired from her journey and soon fell asleep.

Chapter 4.

Early the next morning Fizzy was woken with a start. It was still dark in the shed so she imagined it must still be night time.

Perhaps it's Santa? Perhaps he's come to take me home to the warm kitchen to be with my mum. The shed door opened, and in came Mr Green smiling.

He scooped Fizzy up and put her back into the box which he tied up with a ribbon. *Perhaps he is taking me home to my mum, or perhaps to meet my new family.* Either way, Fizzy was excited, she really hoped she would have an excellent Christmas day!

Mr Green told Fizzy to be quiet, and she tried her best but let out a little whimpering sound, she just couldn't help herself and couldn't decide if she was nervous, excited or frightened.

The box was carried into the house, Fizzy looked out of the tiny hole. The house seemed to be very tidy and warm and Fizzy was happy about this. Room by room they walked through the house and through the hole Fizzy could see a beautiful cream carpet on all the floors, this looked warm to lie on she thought!

They entered an enormous room with a beautiful fireplace, and a gigantic Christmas tree with beautiful red and golden bows on it. It was different to the Christmas tree at her mums house there were no decorations made by the children, there were no decorations made with toilet rolls, or bits of dough, this was indeed, REALLY REALLY REALLY POSH!

Mr Green placed Fizzy's box on the floor beside the sofa. "Happy Christmas." he said to his wife as he bent down to kiss her on the cheek.

"Thank you darling," she said, and pulled open the huge red ribbon and peeked inside the box.
"No," she shouted "No, oh no!"
"What?" said Mr Green.
"You got me a puppy!" she screamed with joy, she sounded really excited as she lifted Fizzy out of the box and placed her on her knee.

Fizzy was excited too, she was so glad to get out of the box and run around this beautiful house with the lovely cream carpet and the red and golden Christmas tree, but in her excitement as she landed on the ladies lap, she couldn't help herself, and did a little wee all over her new mum.

Mrs Green screamed, REALLY LOUDLY! She was very cross as she had her best Christmas dress on and now it was covered in wee. She stood up and put poor Fizzy back into the box.
"Look what it's done!" She wasn't happy, "I'm going to have to get changed and we'll be late for lunch - take it outside to the garden, we can't be late!"

Mr Green scooped Fizzy into his arms, placed her in the box, closed it up again, and took Fizzy out to the garden. He put the box on the floor and opened it up.

"I didn't expect you to do that, you've ruined her dress", he shouted angrily at Fizzy.

Now Fizzy had learnt as a tiny puppy, that if she opened her eyes as widely as she could, lifted her ears as high as they would go, and tilted her head to one side, her family would smile, call her cute and give her heaps of cuddles... it was time to try this trick on Mr Green.

"You can look at me like that as much as you want, but you've just spoilt my surprise," he growled, "You are really cute, but you can't go weeing on people and expecting to get away with it… OFF YOU GO, you'll have to stay in the garden until we've come back from lunch."

Fizzy was sad, her head hung low, her eyes went droopy, her ears fell down to the side of her head, she was so sad in fact, that she worried her tail may never wag again. It was cold and she was tired and very hungry, she missed the warmth of her mums shaggy coat, she missed being tickled behind the ear, and most of all she missed the love of her family.

Fizzy wandered around the garden and found a bush to lie underneath to protect her from the cold mountain winds. She dug a little hole and snuggled into it to try to get some sleep.

I must try harder she thought. *I must not get too excited, I must not wee on Mrs Green's dress, and I need to do my best to look cute* Fizzy kept repeating this to herself. The more she said it the more she could feel the love and warmth of her mother beside her and she drifted off to sleep.

Chapter 5

Mr and Mrs Green returned to the garden late in the day, it was just starting to get dark. Fizzy had slept all afternoon and she woke when she heard them coming through the gate. She jumped up as quickly as she could and ran over to her new human mum as fast as her stubby legs would allow her remembering to keep her eyes wide open; her ears held up as high as she could hold them; her head tilted to one side and, she suddenly remembered that she should wag her tail.

Well, as you will know, when you're little, it's very hard to remember to do everything, and the faster she ran, the more she forgot, by the time she arrived she was out of breath!

Mrs Green bent down to stroke her. Fizzy was so excited to have some love that she jumped up to her getting mud from the garden all over her dress and ruining her clothes for the second time that day.

"Oh NO, bad puppy, bad puppy, look at what you've done!" Mrs Green pushed her away and marched into the house to get changed again.

Mr Green put his hands on his hips and looked down towards Fizzy "You have to do better than that pup," he said as he followed his wife into the house and closed the door behind him.

Fizzy sat alone in the garden. Her happy eyes were full of tears, her ears drooped down and, her tail had lost all of it's energy. She was cold, scared and hungry.

Perhaps Mrs Green would come back out, perhaps she was just getting changed? Then she'd come back, pick her up, stroke her behind her ears just like her real mum had done. To help Mr and Mrs Green to find her easily Fizzy ran to wait at the front door. The step was cold and hard but, this would be the best place to be found so she sat there for what seemed like hours just waiting to make her new family happy.

Some time passed and, the cold mountain winds blew around the doorway. Fizzy could see her own breath in the air, a bit like when you breathe out on a cold winter's day. Finally, Mr Green came to the door with a bowl, he bent down to Fizzy, picked her up and held her under his arms. He carried her to the shed she had slept in last night, opened the door and put the bowl down next to her pink blanket on the floor. He closed the door behind him and left poor Fizzy alone with her bowl of food.

Fizzy was starving, literally starving. Puppies like to eat small amounts of food three or four times a day and that, with her mother's milk, helped her grow strong and healthy. The chunks of meat in the bowl were big and they tasted bitter, even with the sauce on them but, Fizzy didn't care. She ate the food really quickly, so quickly that it made her feel sick.

After a little time her tummy started making gurgling noises as the big pieces of meat she had eaten so quickly, just a short while before, were churning around inside of her.

Poor Fizzy felt so poorly she had to go to bed. Once again, for the second night, she was cold and alone - as she lay in her bed she started to cry. She just wanted her mum back, she wanted to be warm and loved. The more she thought about it, the more she cried. Fizzy cried until out of sheer exhaustion she fell asleep alone on the cold pink rug.

Within just a few hours she was woken by the cold mountain winds rattling the door of the shed. She was wondering if Mr and Mrs Green had forgotten her, surely not, she was there to give them love and make them happy just like mum had explained.

She thought for a while about how she could get attention from her new family, before she would whimper and mum would come running to her. If mum was busy Fizzy worked out that she should bark a bit louder to be heard.

Not knowing how far away Mr and Mrs Green were from the shed and not wanting to be any bother, she started to whimper. She whimpered and whimpered but there was no response. Soon she started to bark, she knew that barking would surely get the family's attention so she barked and she barked as loudly as she possibly could but, no one came. Before Fizzy knew it, her barking turned into more of a howl, this shocked Fizzy, she didn't realise she could make such a big noise - it was quite impressive as she sounded more like a wolf than a puppy dog. She loved the sound she could make. It felt as if this howl was coming from the end of her tail, working all the way through her body and just falling out of her mouth - it was almost as if she was singing. Delighted with this noise, she continued again and again, she was sure this would work and remind her new family that she was there to give love and make them happy.

Finally, Fizzy heard the sound of the door, she stopped to listen, yes, definitely yes, it was the sound of Mr Green's footsteps. They had obviously remembered she was there and waiting to love them. She was sure he would pick her up and lovingly carry her in his arms to the cosy lounge with the Christmas tree and the lovely cream carpet.

Mr Green opened the door. "Shut up pup" he said. "I don't need this from you in the middle of the night, just shut up and behave!" he slammed the door and she heard his footsteps walking away.

Fizzy went back to her bed. Well the howling seemed to work but, still he doesn't want my love thought Fizzy. The howling had made her voice hurt and she was thirsty. She drank from the cold bowl of water that was put down for her the night before, before long she was asleep on the cold pink blanket.

Chapter 6.

Morning came, Fizzy was woken up with a pain in her tummy.

"Oh no, I need a wee, I need a wee, I need a wee" she cried. With the big meal from last night and all the water after the howling, she REALLY needed a wee. Fizzy was stuck in the shed and thought to cry to her new parents for help but, she remembered that it had taken ages last night for them to come to her. She looked around for a place to go to the toilet.

The shed was small, next to the pink blanket on the floor there was a small place with rakes and spades but, no space there to have a wee. Fizzy wandered to the door, and decided this would be the most convenient place to go to the toilet. Being right by the door it would show her new family that she tried to get out to go and, they surely wouldn't mind especially when they knew how much she was going to love them.

"Puppy, Puppy"! Cried Mrs Green.
Yes my new mum is here, she's remembered me, "Yes yes, I'm here, I'm here" said Fizzy barking.

Mrs Green opened the door and Fizzy ran out to greet her so excited to give her some love at last! Fizzy paused for a second, eyes, ears, tilt the head, wag my tail, give love, "I'm ready!"

"Ah puppy, you terror, you kept us awake all night, but it's lovely to be greeted like this!" said Mrs Green.

Fizzy remembered her mother's words, and pulled the cutest of faces possible. As Mrs Green bent down to stroke her, Fizzy ran through her legs in excitement, *I will love you, I will listen to you, I will be beside you forever* thought Fizzy showing her as best as she could how delighted she was she was there.

Mrs Green pulled the strangest of faces, "Oh, erk, you smell bad, you need a bath" she said, lifting her hand to her nose, "Hold on there, I'll go and sort something out."

Fizzy wasn't too sure what a bath was, she knew when she smelt bad that her mum licked her to make her clean, will Mrs Green do the same?

Mrs Green scurried away and came back with a yellow bottle, a towel, and a long green thing that looked like a snake. Perhaps it was a game, perhaps Fizzy should put it in her mouth and run around with this just like she did with her brothers and sisters with the puppy toys they had. But the green thing was strange, it had water coming out of it. Fizzy went up to inspect, she was thirsty, she had finished all the water in the shed through the night. The water was icy cold and Fizzy jumped back as it was far too cold to drink.

Mrs Green placed the items in a bucket on the floor with the green hose running water into a nearby drain, and reached into her pocket. From inside, she pulled out a sparkling pink collar with shiny jewels on it. Fizzy had never seen anything as beautiful before, it was prettier than the Christmas tree and certainly very pink! She bent down beside Fizzy and put the collar towards her neck. Fizzy again remembered to open her eyes wide with love, tip her ears forwards to be attentive and tilt her head to the side for cuteness. As she did Mrs Green put her arms around her neck, her hands tickled behind Fizzy's ear reminding Fizzy of the time just a few days before when her real mum had licked there. It tickled so much, what a kind thing for Mrs Green to do she thought. It made Fizzy squirm and run, this was a fun game.

"Stop, stand still puppy, wait" yelled Mrs Green as Fizzy darted off in the direction of the bucket. The hose pipe that was leaning on it was nudged out of the way and flew into the air sending water spraying all over yet another set of clean clothes.

"No, really? This can't be happening! I didn't want you anyway, now you stink and I'm covered in freezing water, well stuff you, you can stay smelly in the garden, you're not coming in my house until you're clean!" Mrs Green stormed off whilst Fizzy sat practising her cute look that should melt the heart of any loving family.

Mrs Green slammed the door as she raced into the house. Fizzy thought she should follow her to comfort her and remind her that she was there to love her. As luck would have it the door hadn't closed properly and there was a Fizzy sized gap that she could use to enter the house.

Fizzy pushed the door open with her nose and looked inside. She saw a long corridor in front of her with a set of stairs to her right but, there was noone to be seen. Dogs noses work better than human noses and it was just at this point when Fizzy smelt the most amazing smell. It wasn't a pretty smell but, a tasty smell and Fizzy's attention was taken by this. You may have heard the saying to follow your nose, I'm pretty sure this comes from the fact, that dogs always seem to follow their noses!

And so Fizzy followed the tasty smell, she passed the doorway to the left with the beautiful Christmas tree she had admired the day before, she went through the hallway and at the very end was an open door which, she went through. There were cupboards and shelves all around the sides of the room, and a large table in the middle with seats around it. She was in the kitchen, though it wasn't like her old kitchen.This was all very shiney and new, with not a dogs bed in sight!

Fizzy, being a stumpy variety of dog, couldn't reach up onto the chairs but, there was definitely something interesting up there, and whatever it was, it smelt very good. Fizzy walked around the edge of the table several times but, there was no way up. She wandered out of the kitchen back through the hallway and into the lounge where she had been the day before.

Fizzy sat and gazed in awe at the beauty of the red and golden tree. She knew she had to be big and brave away from mum and knew that her real mum would be so happy to see her with her beautiful tree in her lovely house on the soft cream carpet.

Oops, Fizzy looked down, beneath her paws was the beautiful cream carpet and as she lifted one paw she saw the mud print she had left. She raised the other paw and yes, as you would suspect, there was another mud print. Never mind she thought, I'll just warm myself up and make myself comfy beside the fire.

It was some hours later that Mrs Green found her there whilst coming downstairs, in yet another change of clothes. She spotted muddy paw marks on her clean cream carpet, following the trail, she walked into the kitchen, around the table, back out into the hallway and into the lounge where to her horror she found the culprit - Fizzy fast asleep beside the fire.

Mrs Green yelled. Fizzy was in a very deep sleep, she was dreaming of times snuggled with her mother whilst watching her brothers and sisters playing, remembering the warm and comforting feeling of nuzzling into her fur and then, BANG...

"Get out, get out you wretched dog, get out of my house!" Fizzy jumped up startled, she tried with all her might to put on her cute face but was terrified of Mrs Green standing there bashing the carpet beside her with a broom. Tucking her tail under her body she made for the door as fast as her stubby legs could carry her and escaped out into the cold before the door slammed shut behind her.

Fizzy looked back. *That didn't go so well* she thought, *I didn't even have the time to show Mrs Green the love, attention and devotion I should have shown her. Now she's angry and I just don't know why!*

Fizzy spent the next few days with her new family much as she had the first two, banned from the house, left in the cold, and shut in the cold dark shed at night.

Chapter 7.

It was lonely in the garden. On one day Fizzy saw a robin on the lawn dancing on the ground with his feet and pecking with his beak. She raced over to ask the bird what he was doing but, he flew off leaving Fizzy and the worm alone. Wanting to inspect it further she dug a little hole in the grass, the worm went further and further into the ground and, as it did, she scraped further and further at the mud. The worm had disappeared deep into the soil, before she knew it she had dug a rather impressive hole. Mr and Mrs Green were not pleased and, as punishment, Fizzy spent the afternoon in the shed.

On another occasion Fizzy's teeth were hurting. Being a puppy they loose their teeth and grow new ones just like we do but, this can sometimes be really painful. It helps for puppies to have something to chew on. Fizzy came across an interesting object rather like a vine that grows grapes. Being winter there were no leaves on the vine. I it was a really interesting plant as it twisted up over an old metal archway.

As Fizzy chewed on the long wooded vine it made the archway wobble and creak, she pulled it further to investigate what would happen. Over a very little time she got to the end of the vine. It came crashing down into the garden taking with it the old rustic effect archway, frankly thought Fizzy it will do them a favour - it was very old and very creaky. The Greens didn't see the funny side when they returned home from work and again Fizzy spent the night in the dark shed as punishment.

The problem with the dark shed was that Fizzy couldn't see too much, there wasn't much room to move around in there and, certainly nowhere suitable to go to the toilet. Being a small puppy with a small bladder she did need to go on regular occasions. Every time she would go to the toilet in the shed she would get into trouble.

Poor Fizzy was very sad, very lonely and very confused. Why couldn't her new family accept her love? Did they just not want it? Did they just not have time for it? Was she not opening her eyes wide enough? Bending her ears forward enough? Tipping her head to one side enough? She was still working on the tail wagging bit but, quite frankly, it was enough to try to be cute without having to co-ordinate the tail wagging too. In reality she honestly didn't feel much like wagging her tail although she tried her best.

Chapter 8.

One morning, as with every morning, she heard Mr Green walking towards her shed to let her out. Only this morning something was different. As he opened the shed door he blocked it with his foot. Fizzy was used to running out into the garden to do her morning wee but, this time she couldn't get past and bashed her nose on the toe of his boot.

"Come on pup," he said, "It's time to go."

Where are we going? wondered Fizzy, *Are we going in to the house with the cream coloured carpet?*

Are we going home to my real mum with the warm bed beside the fire, and the licks that tickle me behind my ear?

Mr Green scooped her up and put her into a rather smart cage. The cage had a plastic bottom, and metal sides that she could see through, this was far better than the Christmas box she arrived in.

Mr Green placed the cage into the car on the back seat and he drove off with Fizzy. The drive was quite long and the car slipped on the icy roads. Fizzy got quite hot in the back, there were no windows open and she couldn't decide if, after all, it was better to feel cold.

Fizzy was startled when the car stopped. Mr Green opened the door and picked up Fizzy's cage. Fizzy could hear the sound of lots of dogs barking, they didn't sound like the happiest of barks, but hey… perhaps they were dog friends. She was carried into a big office area and put on a long desk covered in papers.

"We can't keep her, she's messy, she's not house trained and she jumps up at people," Fizzy overheard Mr Green, "Besides she's ruined the garden, and the carpets in the house."

Fizzy was perplexed! She wasn't aware that the garden was ruined, it was indeed a very fine garden, and she'd grown fond of it over the past few days. As for the carpet, she had hardly been in the house apart from that fateful day when the water was cold and got splashed everywhere.

Fizzy looked around the room. There were some kind looking people and on the floor there was a big scary dog with a muzzle on him. He had a big black collar and kept lurching forwards towards a sweet looking tabby cat on the floor. His human was shouting at him and pulling backwards on his lead.

Fizzy loved cats. At the house where she was born, there were three of them, they were always trying to break into the house and they loved her mum who would repeatedly open the door to let them in. The cats would jump up onto the surfaces in the kitchen and knock down the occasional dinner or tasty snack that the humans had left on the side.

Tabby cat looked up towards Fizzy and then jumped on the table beside her for a closer inspection, "Another one that can't behave, eugh, and a puppy too. We don't need more puppies in here!" she said.

"But aside from that, I'd like to welcome you, my name is Tabby, and I'm the boss around here, any problems just come to me."

"Good morning," said Fizzy, tilting her head to one side "Nice to meet you."

"You too. You're the fifth puppy who has come in this week but, you're short and stumpy - it will take you ages to find a home! These days they want big dogs, shiny black ones, labradors, proper big dogs, little stumpy ones have no place in modern homes. If people wanted a short dog they'd get a pedigree not some tatty tiny misbehaving puppy like you! What kind of dog are you even? Look at that enormously long body, those big paws, and those stubby legs. You don't even look like a real dog!"

Fizzy looked down at herself, she'd not really thought about the fact that she was disproportionate before. Her mum told her she had lovely little legs and a beautiful long body - she looked just like mum, and mum was indeed beautiful.

Before she realised it a pair of lovely smelling hands entered her cage and picked her up. Fizzy was too busy looking around to remember to look at the lady with her cute eyes and listen intently with her ears. She was just about to reply to Tabby the cat when she was taken down a long corridor and placed into a room.

The room smelt of other dogs, Fizzy looked up to see three puppies running towards her. As with every dog Fizzy would meet in her life, they were all much bigger and much more boisterous!

One puppy had a rope in his mouth, another had her hair tied up in a bow on the top of her head, and the final one, a big shaggy puppy, raced towards her and threw herself at Fizzy knocking her to the floor.

 "Oops sorry" she said, "I was so excited to see a new friend, I forgot my manners."

Fizzy was pleased to meet new friends, though a little disconcerted to have them sniffing at her bum. (It's a dog thing)!

The puppies raced around the room showing off and playing tag with the rope, tormenting each other, whilst Fizzy sat in awe of their confidence. On the other side of the room was a warm and welcoming bed, she was confused and exhausted, and decided to go and take a nap.

A short while later there was the clanging of gates and the most intense noise of dogs barking, it was loud and very scarey for Fizzy who looked up from her bed.

"Quick, quick, it's selection time," said the big tatty haired puppy who had knocked her over earlier.

Fizzy was too scared to move and watched from her bed as a young couple with their daughter walked up to the bars in front of the room they were in. They bent down at the bars and talked to the puppies that were in the room and, before long, a lady opened the door and picked up the crazy puppy who was playing earlier with the rope.

The puppy was taken away, the other puppies turned around and headed back to the assortments of beds at the back their heads low and their tails looking sad.

Chapter 9.

Over the next few days the puppies all left Fizzy, they told her they were going to new families and wished her luck. Fizzy was the last puppy left, she was alone and sad but, found an unlikely friendship with Tabby the resident cat who would pop by daily and squeeze through the bars of the room.

Tabby would come by three times a day to help feed all the dogs and in the evening, she would stop to chat and hide with Fizzy so that she wouldn't be put out into the cold for the night. They would cuddle up and Tabby would tell her stories of the previous puppies and how they found homes. She'd tell tales of the world outside the little room, of the dinners she stole, and the sun that was shining but, Fizzy remained sad and pining for love.

Every day an assortment of people would walk past her room and look in at her. She would lie quietly in her bed and look up but, she was so sad she couldn't find the energy or motivation to walk to the bars or look cute.

Tabby felt she had to have words with Fizzy, if Fizzy couldn't cheer up and look cute she'd never find a family. Before she knew it she wouldn't be a cute puppy and she would be an adult dog. Many of Tabby's adult dog friends had been in the shelter for months and some even for years. Something HAD to be done!

"Fizzy, outside of here, there's a big wide world. There are fields to run through, mountains to climb, forests to explore! Somewhere out there there is a family who will love you who have a warm bed and lovely children to play with. Somewhere, there is a family who won't judge you on your stubby legs and your ridiculously long body, they'll want you to be part of their family because you have a kind heart and cute eyes."

Fizzy looked up at Tabby and Tabby licked her just behind the ear! It tickled and Fizzy started to giggle, it reminded her of her time with mum, the gentleness and kindness she had experienced with her family and the warmth of the love she felt and the wisdom of her mother's words.

Fizzy's sparkle came back into her eyes.

"Fizzy, your eyes sparkle with such love, you really should use those eyes to get attention," said Tabby.

Fizzy's ears perked up and dropped forward in a cute attentive way, just like her mother had shown her.

"Oh Fizzy," said Tabby " Look at those ears, they're the cutest ever, you look so intelligent and adorable."

Fizzy tipped her head to one side…

"Oh Fizzy," Tabby pushed her head into Fizzy's face to give her a special cat kiss.

"Fizzy, you may not be a pedigree, you may not be a big shiny dog and you do have the stumpiest legs in the world but, your heart and soul shine through all of that. You just need to show the families that visit what a wonderful heart you have."

Just then, a family with a little blond haired boy walked past Fizzy remembered her tail and she stood up to wag. She ran over to the bars to greet them opening her eyes as wide as they would go and staring straight into the little boys eyes. The boy bent down to stroke Fizzy and she jumped up at the bars to greet him keeping her eyes fixated on his, her ears up and attentive to him, her face tilted to one side.

The boy called his dad over "Oh Dad, please can we take this one home, she's lovely."

"I thought we wanted a BIG dog, that one is tiny and she's not going to grow much at all!" said Dad, "I thought you wanted one you could play ball with and take out on long walks in the forest? No Elliot, let's go, let's look for a big dog that can keep up with you."

"But Dad, she's adorable." said Elliot looking up to his father.

Fizzy stretched up towards the young boy, standing on her back feet and placing her paws on the bars between them. She continued to stare intently into the boy's eyes, lifting her eyebrows up as far as she could to make her eyes bigger.

"Keep going, work it, work it, don't forget that tail," said Tabby from the back of the room. "Don't let this boy go, he (like you) has a kind heart."

"Dad" said Elliot, "Actually, no, I know I wanted a big dog but this isn't any ordinary dog just look at how her eyes sparkle. She's not just a dog, she's going to be a special friend!"

Dad bent down. Fizzy's eyebrows were hurting from holding them up to make her eyes big, she sat down on the other side of the bars and focussed on tilting her head - just a little to start with and then a little more!

"I see what you mean, she does look like a kind soul," he said, "She's very pretty and looks like she'll be a loyal friend but, goodness only knows what breed she is or how big she'll get with those stubby legs."

Before Fizzy knew what was happening, she was picked up by the kind lady in the shelter and placed in Elliots arms.

By the end of the day she was in her new home, sharing her love with her new family.

… the story does not end there! No, in fact, it's only just started.

A wonderful thing about this story is that Fizzy, in real life, has arrived at Elliots farm. She's living with Farmer Zac and has three other wonderful furry dog friends. Fizzy has a huge sofa to lie on, a bed beside a warm fire and not only that, Tabby the cat came with her too. You see, this isn't just a true story that has a beginning a middle and an end. It's a real story with a real puppy (now called Fizzy Pop), it's about the beginning of a life adventure and now you can meet Fizzy for yourself.

The next part of Fizzy's story is a short film of her life and adventures, published on Youtube on the 20th December 2017, be sure to follow her and see how her life unfolds.

Fizzy thought back to her mums words… "Then my children, with your wide eyes looking straight at each other to show love, and your lifted ears to show you're listening, you then tip your head to the side so show that you're cute and that you care about people. This shows the kindness in you, it shows off your heart and your love and will help you find a wonderful new family."

Here is Fizzy Pop. Happy living on her farm with Elliot and Farmer Zac. She has lots of dogs and other animals to play with, and spends her days running around the farm with her friends, who include; Carla the pig, Domdom the llama, Maple the mountain dog, Marjorie the duck, Maya the sheep, Panda the alpaca and many many more!

Farmer Zac tells beautiful stories of the events that happen at the farm, look out for his books and his many tales.

Follow Fizzy on Instagram - Fizzypop_the_rescue_dog

"Fizzy, outside of here, there's a big wide world. There are fields to run through, mountains to climb, forests to explore! Somewhere out there there is a family who will love you who have a warm bed and lovely children to play with. Somewhere, there is a family who won't judge you on your stubby legs and your ridiculously long body, they'll want you to be part of their family because you have a kind heart and cute eyes." (Tabby, February 2017)

Printed in Great Britain
by Amazon